by Anna Kang *illustrated by* Christopher Weyant

That's (Not) Mine

SCHOLASTIC INC.

*To our parents for their loving support
and for teaching us how to share.*

ISBN 978-1-338-10113-3

12 11 10 9 8 7 6 5   17 18 19 20 21

Printed in the U.S.A.   40

First Scholastic printing, September 2016

Design by Sara Gillingham Studio
The illustrations are rendered in ink and watercolor with brush pens on Arches paper.

That's my chair.

No, it's mine.

I was sitting in it before.

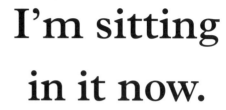

I'm sitting in it now.

TICKLE
TICKLE

Want to
go play?

Yeah!

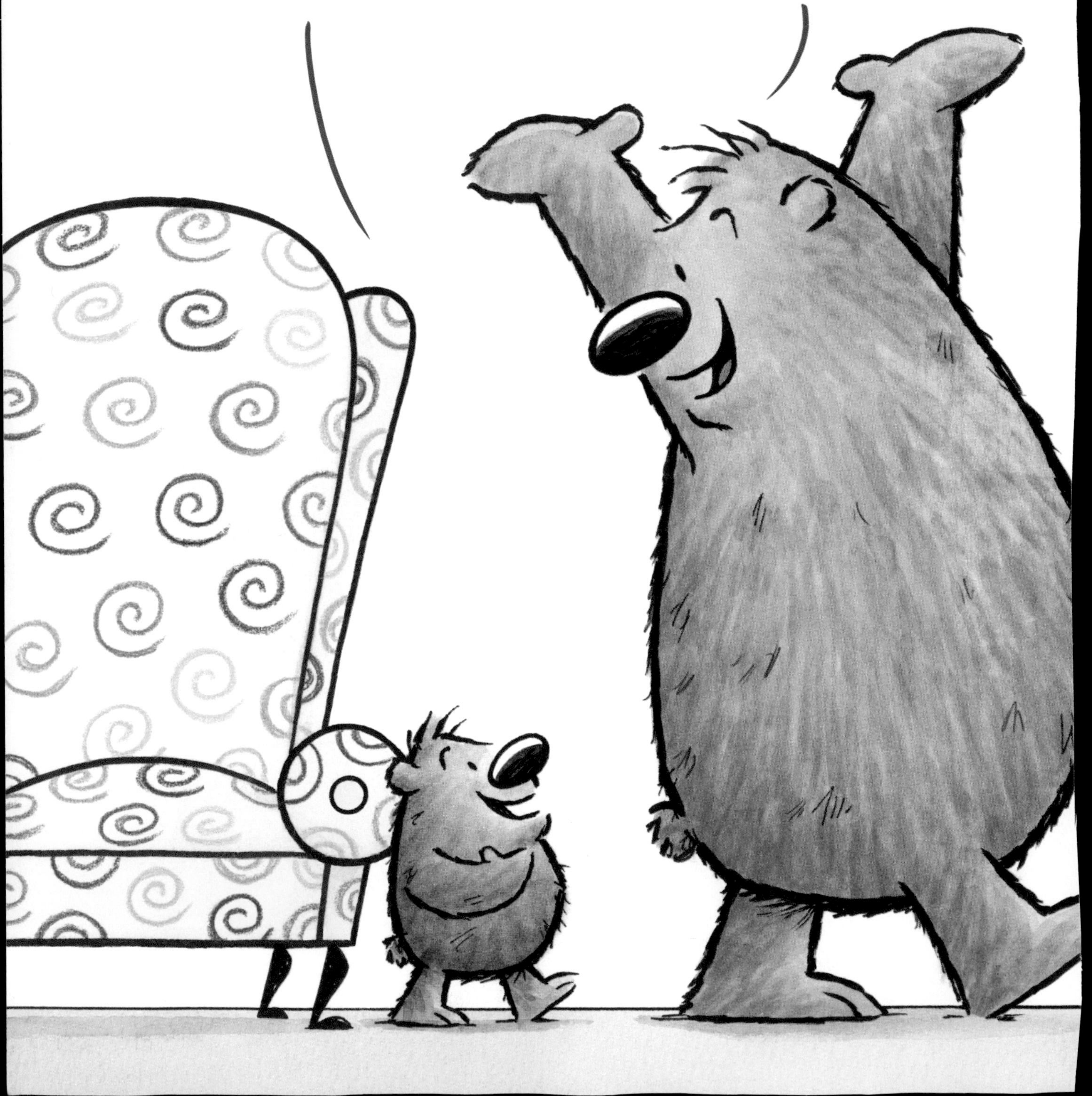